The Sleeping Beauty

Retold by Ian Robinson
Illustrated by Gerry Embleton

Printed in Belgium

ISBN 0 86163 010 6
© Award Publications Ltd. 1980
Spring House, Spring Place,
London NW5, England

Once upon a time, there lived a king and queen who were loved by all their subjects and, although they were very happy, they dearly wanted a child.

Imagine the rejoicing in the kingdom, when at last the Queen gave birth to a baby daughter. The King immediately declared a public holiday, bells rang out from every steeple in the land and everybody was invited to a christening party for the little Princess.

The guests of honour at the party were to be seven good fairies who would give the child their special blessings. To celebrate the occasion, the King ordered his jeweller to make seven beautiful gold caskets which were to be set at each of the fairy's places in the banqueting hall.

The day of the christening arrived and all the guests began to assemble in the hall.

"This is the happiest moment of my life!" the King whispered to the Queen and kissed her on the cheek.

Just as the ceremonies began, there was a noise at the back of the hall and an ugly old woman walked boldly up to the King.

"So! You were about to start without me, were you?" she cried.

At this the crowd were very surprised — the old woman was a fairy who lived all by herself far away in the wild woods. It was such a long time since anyone had seen her that the King and Queen had forgotten to invite her to the christening!

"How can I tell how sorry I am," said the King; "do come and sit with us." At this the old woman seemed happier; she sat down with the King and the banquet started.

When the meal was over, it was time for the fairies to give the Princess their blessings.

"My present is the gift of song," said the first,

"may the little Princess sing as sweetly as a nightingale on a summer's evening."

"May she be as fair as a rose and as fresh as the morning dew," added the second.

"May her eye be as sharp as a hawk's and her mind as quick as silver."

"May she ride like the wind and dance like a lamb in the springtime," said the fourth, while the fifth wished her silken hair and the laughter of a mountain brook and the sixth promised her long life and happiness.

The old woman suddenly rose to her feet and uttered a terrible curse.

"All your fine words won't save this child from my vengeance!" she hissed. "All your silly blessings have been in vain, for on the very first time she sees a spinning wheel, the Princess will prick her finger and die!"

Everybody was dismayed to hear the old woman's words. The Queen hugged her baby while the King tried to comfort her as best he could — it was of no use, the Princess was doomed to die.

But at that moment, the seventh good fairy, who had hidden herself away at the sight of the woman, stepped forward and spoke softly to the King and Queen.

"Alas, I cannot undo the evil which has been done," she said, "but I can change the spell with my own blessing for the Princess. She will *not* die when she pricks her finger, but will fall asleep for a hundred years, only to be woken by a prince from distant lands."

Although the King was overjoyed that his daughter was spared from death, he set out to make sure that no part of the bad fairy's curse should ever come true. A proclamation was read in every village; every spinning wheel in the kingdom was to be destroyed. All over the land they were piled high in the market squares and armed soldiers were told to make sure that every last one was burned to a cinder.

The years passed and the little Princess grew up to be a beautiful young girl, just as the good fairies foretold. The King and Queen were delighted to see her playing happily in the castle gardens and to hear her sweet singing drift through the cloisters. Surely no harm could ever befall

such a charming and delightful young creature?

One day, when she was exploring the castle cellars, the Princess came to a little door she had never seen before. She pushed it open, and finding a staircase on the other side, decided to climb it to see where it could lead.

As she reached the top of the stairs, the Princess saw one of the oddest sights she had ever seen. There, surrounded by coloured wools, sat an old lady spinning.

"Hello, my dear, come in," said the old lady when she saw the Princess, "come here and sit beside me." The Princess was fascinated by the spinning wheel at which the old woman sat.

"Whatever are you doing?" she asked.

"Why, spinning, of course," the old lady replied. "When I was a girl everyone could do it; now this must be the only spinning wheel left in the whole kingdom."

"Oh, do let me try!" pleaded the Princess, "it looks such fun, I'm sure you could show me what to do."

"Of course," replied the old lady and she sat the Princess down at the wheel where she started to spin. No sooner had she begun to take up the wool from the spindle, however, than she pricked her finger and fell to the ground in a deep, deep sleep.

At this the old woman let out a horrible peal of laughter.

"That will teach them to think they can outwit me!" she cried. The old woman was none other than the bad fairy in disguise — she had got her revenge at last!

When he heard the terrible news, the King was very upset. Sadly, he carried his daughter to the Royal Chambers and laid her to rest. All through the night he sat by her side in the cold, dark room, tears trickling down his cheeks.

At last, news of the terrible fate which had befallen the Princess reached the good fairy who had saved her life at her christening. She hurried to the castle at once to see the King and Queen.

"How unlucky it is that you should live to see this day," she said, "I cannot see you parted from your daughter so cruelly; if she is to sleep for a hundred years, then you and the court must do the same." As she spoke, the good fairy blew magic dust into their eyes, and the King and Queen felt themselves growing weary. Soon they fell asleep exactly as they were, sitting in front of the Princess's bed.

When the King and Queen were soundly asleep, the fairy flew from room to room scattering her magic dust wherever she went. Maids, grooms, soldiers and serving boys fell asleep where they stood and silence fell over the castle.

In the great hall the jester had just started to tell a joke when the fairy's spell sent him to sleep. The musicians fell into a deep slumber still holding their instruments, and the chancellor and the magician, who were playing a game of chess,

began to snore loudly as
if both were tired of
waiting for the other to
finish his turn. Out in the
courtyard the stable lads
fell asleep as they were
sweeping and even the
horses dozed in their stalls.

At last, when everyone in the whole castle was soundly asleep, the good fairy cast a final spell.

"You will all sleep safely for a hundred years until the Princess wakens from her slumbers." she whispered and then she made a mighty forest of briars grow up around the whole castle, all but hiding it from view, so that only the topmost towers could be seen.

So the castle remained for a hundred years. People came and went past the enchanted wood which surrounded its mighty walls and strange stories about the fate which had befallen it spread far and wide. The woods were said by some to be haunted, and people soon started to hurry past the castle as fast as their legs could carry them.

Word of the mysterious castle reached a handsome young prince from a far-away land across the sea, who was determined to see it for himself and to take the beautiful princess, mentioned in the story, for his bride.

After many days journeying, the Prince came to the tangled wood of brambles and briars.

"I am not afraid of old stories!" he told himself and started to hack aside the thorny bushes with his sword. To his astonishment, suddenly a pathway opened in the woods before him. As if by magic he found himself being led deeper and deeper through the forest, until he found himself standing before the castle walls.

Once inside the castle gate the Prince gave out a cry of amazement, for there before him, looking as though they had fallen asleep that very afternoon, lay the servants of the castle. Tools lay scattered around them; there sat a man peeling apples, there a maid with a broom sleeping on the stairs.

"This must indeed be some strange and marvellous magic!" exclaimed the Prince, rubbing his eyes in disbelief. He took up a candle-stick from the table and began to climb the stairs to the Royal apartments. As he entered the Royal Chamber, his heart gave a wild leap for before him, exactly as the old story had foretold, lay the most beautiful girl he had ever seen — the sleeping Princess.

Slowly the Prince drew nearer the bed where the sleeping beauty lay. Bending gently over her silent form, he kissed her lightly on the lips. Suddenly her eyelids fluttered and the Princess began to stretch. After all those years, the good fairy's final wish had come true. The Princess awoke and saw standing before her the handsome young Prince who had broken the spell and set her free. They fell in love at once and the Prince vowed to make her his bride.

As soon as the spell was broken, people began to wake up all over the palace. The King and Queen guessed at once what had happened and immediately gave the young couple their blessing. The sound of music and laughter came from the great hall, whilst the jester finished telling his joke.

"Your move!" cried the chancellor to the
magician, and then they were dancing and
singing and making merry. The forest
around the castle vanished, the flags of
the kingdom flew proud and clear in the breeze
and messengers rode out from the palace to
tell everybody what had happened.

When the wonderful news spread across the land, people came from every corner of the kingdom to welcome back the wise old King and to celebrate the marriage of the Prince and Princess. The King and Queen wept with joy to see their daughter once again so happy and everyone said what a fine pair the young couple made.

After the wedding the Prince and his bride set sail for his castle across the sea. When they arrived, everybody was charmed and delighted with the beautiful Princess and they both lived happily ever after.